Meet the PIKMI POPS

By Sydney Malone

ISBN 978-1-338-31604-9

10 9 8 7 6 5 4 3 2 1 18 19 20 21 22

Printed in the U.S.A. 40

First printing 2018

Book design by Becky James

SCHOLASTIC INC.

Pikmi Land is full of the sweetest animals around!

The Pikmis who live there come in all the colors of the rainbow. Some Pikmis smell like juicy fruits and some smell like sweet desserts. Some are talkative and others are shy. Some fly in the air and some dig in the ground. But every Pikmi is a great friend, and they all love to spend time together! Which Pikmi is your favorite?

Read all about them to find out!

Dream the Unicorn

Dream is one adorable explorer who loves to try anything new. This golden-horned unicorn is always running through rainbows to add color to its coat!

All about Dream

Scent: Marshmallow
Quote: "Let's go chase some rainbows!"
Favorite Treat: Marshmallow
Likes: Rainbow sliding

Ebby the Bunny

Ebby can bounce around like a bubble. This bunny just has to be careful it doesn't pop and end up in a sticky situation!

All about Ebby

Scent: Bubblegum
Quote: "You're a bun of fun!"
Hobbies: Blowing bubbles and juggling
Favorite Treat: Bubblegum breakfasts

Tubble the Goat

Tubble is a goat who eats anything sweet! This Pikmi's diet may not be balanced, but when it's dancing, nothing makes this goat tumble. Tubble is one sure-footed sweet tooth!

Fuwa the Fox

Fuwa the Fox is very tricky. You'll see this Pikmi's tail popping over the hills—but catching it is a different story! But when you do finally meet, you'll become friends for life!

All about Fuwa

Scent: Raspberry
Quote: "Together fur ever!"
Favorite Treat: Lemonade lollipops
Favorite Pastime: Swinging on the flying fox

Flubb the Pufferfish

Like anyone, Flubb has ups and downs—but mostly ups! Nothing puffs up this pufferfish more than having fun! Flubb can't control it—every time this Pikmi gets excited, it's grow time!

All about Flubb

Scent: Banana
Quote: "Hope your day is swell!"
Favorite Treat: Banana bubblegum
Favorite Pastime: Making balloon animals

Pichi the Dog

Pichi loves surprising others by popping out of the holes it digs! Pichi loves the color blue so much that it even smells like blueberries! If someone is feeling blue, Pichi does whatever it takes to make them laugh. That is what makes Pichi such a doggone good friend.

All about Pichi

Scent: **Blueberry**
Quote: **"Don't worry! Be yappy!"**
Favorite color: **Blue**
Likes: **Digging for blueberry bones**
Favorite Treat: **Blueberry bones, of course**

Snowy the Polar Bear

Snowy adores the cold weather and is always singing and dancing when there's a blizzard. This cool bear is famous for performing on the ice stage. This Pikmi loves being in "*snow*biz"!

All about Snowy

Scent: Caramel apple
Quote: "You're so cool!"
Hobby: Singing in the snow
Favorite Treat: Caramel apple icy pops

Rhubarb the Kangaroo

Rhubarb is a smart roo and doesn't stop thinking about the future. This Pikmi carries watermelon seeds in its pouch and plants them wherever it goes! That way, Rhubarb can have watermelon anytime, anywhere!

All about Rhubarb

Scent: Watermelon
Quote: "I couldn't be hoppier with you!"
Hobby: Boomerang juggling
Favorite Treat: Watermelon waffles

Erkle the Turtle

Erkle the Turtle is a shy little Pikmi who doesn't like to come out of its shell. Everything Erkle needs is on its back. But once this shy Pikmi decides to poke its head out, the fun really begins!

All about Erkle

Scent: Banana
Quote: "Let's shell-ebrate!"
Likes: Watching *shell*evision
Favorite Treat: Peaches and cream

Bibble the Lamb

Bibble is one of the most thoughtful Pikmis. This little lamb uses its own wool to knit beautiful creations. Bibble makes scarves, sweaters, socks, hats, and more snuggly things as gifts for the other Pikmis. Giving gifts is the baaa-st!

All about Bibble

Scent: Vanilla bean marshmallow
Quote: "You're woolly wonderful!"
Hobby: Knitting
Favorite Treat: Marshmallow pudding

Gizmit the Guinea Pig

Like a mini lawn mower, Gizmit the Guinea Pig is always hunting around for the sweetest grass to eat! Come over for lunch one day and share a *hay*burger. A good meal is always better with friends!

All about Gizmit

Scent: Caramel

Quote: "You're a real squeak-heart!"

Favorite Treat: Caramel creams

Favorite Pastime: Having sweet dreams

Mani the Moose

Mani has an amazing imagination and never stops creating fun inventions for the other Pikmis. Mani's job is to put a smile on everyone's face—and this moose does it so well!

All about Mani

Scent: Mint choc chip
Quote: "You're so a-moosing!"
Favorite Treat: Choc mint *moo*sli
Favorite Pastime: Growing organic food

Tater the Golden Retriever

Tater loves looking for treasure in the yard. This Pikmi spends hours digging holes and is always on the hunt for those rare banana bones.

All about Tater

Scent: Banana
Quote: "Your friendship is golden!"
Likes: Drawing treasure maps
Favorite Treat: Banana bones

Glama the Peacock

Glama the Peacock is always putting on a show and loves giving fashion advice to the other Pikmis. Glama's motto is: Be proud of yourself!

All about Glama

Scent: Blueberry
Quote: "So proud to be your friend!"
Favorite Treat: Blueberry and birdseed pies
Favorite Pastime: Showing off great style

Fetti the Cat

This colorful kitty is always merry when it's eating raspberries. No matter where the day takes Fetti, this Pikmi is sure to spreads smiles—and red footprints!—wherever it goes!

Smorey the Dog

Smorey has a heart for art! This creative pup is always surprising friends by making sweet art from the tastiest treats. It's art that's good enough to eat!

Bobble the Budgie

Bobble loves talking. This budgie can chirp in five different languages, which is very handy when it goes migrating to warmer countries in winter.

All about Bobble

Scent: Banana
Quote: "You're the tweetest friend I know!"
Likes: Spending time on Twitter
Favorite Treat: Banana-flavored birdseed

Skittle the Llama

Skittle is always calm and will do anything for anyone. This llama is all about peace and likes to give advice about life to others. Some Pikmis call Skittle the "Dalai Llama"! There's nothing a sweet snack and some calming words can't solve!

All about Skittle

Scent: Cotton candy
Quote: "I'm your 'no-drama' llama!"
Favorite Treat: Cotton candy cornflakes
Favorite Pastime: Meditating under the cotton candy tree

Leroy the Monkey

This monkey loves bananas so much, it's starting to become one! However, Leroy's scent is very a-peeling.

All about Leroy

Scent: Banana
Quote: "You're the pick of the bunch!"
Favorite Treat: Banana-flavored ANYTHING
Favorite Pastime: Banana-skin skating

Chata the Parrot

Chata the Parrot is always on the phone talking to friends. If you want the gossip going around Pikmi Pop Land, just ask this chatterbox.

All about Chata

Scent: Ripe raspberries
Quote: "You're my berry bestie!"
Favorite Treat: Raspberry seed salad
Favorite Pastime: Talking, chatting, speaking, and having conversations

Selby the Sloth

Selby the Sloth has plenty of time for everyone. Pikmis rush to get in line for one of Selby's hugs, which last for ages. It's certainly worth the wait!

All about Selby

Scent: Blueberry
Quote: "You're slow amazing!"
Favorite Treat: Blueberry muffins
Favorite Pastime: Racing snails

Ollie the Bear

Ollie the Bear sleeps on a bubblegum mattress. It's so sweet and comfortable—until it pops!

All about Ollie

Scent: Bubblegum
Quote: "I'll always be bear for you!"
Favorite Treats: Bubblegum and honey sandwiches
Favorite Pastime: Bear-back riding